BRINGING SCHOOL HOME

This book is dedicated to Eric Greer

BRINGING SCHOOL HOME

Children and parents learning together

Ruth Merttens • Jeff Vass

Hodder & Stoughton
LONDON SYDNEY AUCKLAND TORONTO

In this book we have generally referred to your child as 'she' simply to avoid clumsy constructions of 'she/he', 'her/him', and 'herself/himself'.

British Library Cataloguing in Publication Data
Merttens, Ruth
Bringing School home: Children and parents learning together. – (The impact parent book)
1. Education. Participation of parents
I. Title II. Vass, Jeff III. Series
371.103

ISBN 0–340–54085–0

First published 1990

Typeset by Taurus Graphics, Abingdon.
Printed for the educational publishing division of Hodder & Stoughton, Mill Road, Dunton Green, Sevenoaks, Kent by Thomson Litho Ltd, East Kilbride.

Contents

ACKNOWLEDGEMENTS

This book relies upon the experiences of working on IMPACT over the last five years. It could not have been written without the help and support of all the teachers, parents and children who make IMPACT, and all such initiatives, work. We should make a special mention of Alwyn Morgan in Humberside, Ian Lewis and Liz Byard in Gwent, Pat Brown in Barnet, David Owen and Margaret Williams in Devon, Mark Gill and Robin Aldridge in Nottinghamshire, David Bristow in Redbridge, Ann Murray and Paul Latham in Wirral, and Tim Brighouse, Ros Leather and Richard Border in Oxfordshire. Without the support of people like this, home involvement remains a matter of lip-service only.

On a more personal level, love and thanks owed to Deborah Curle and Ian Merttens who have provided constant tea, sympathy and advice (a dangerous practice!). We owe a special debt of gratitude to our own parents Phyllida and Jim Tester, and Barbara and Brian Vass.

Finally, we should thank Harry, Hilda, Fred, Annie, Wilf and Matthew who have allowed their names to be taken in vain. No one gets a chance to practise being a parent and so we learn on our children.

Introduction

It is now recognised by teachers, headteachers and educationists at all levels that parents have a role to play in their children's education. Exactly what is this role? How do parents know how to play it? Who writes the script? What are the rules of the game?

This book is not asking parents to be their child's best, or even first, teacher. It is not looking to parents to 'teach' at all. Neither is it showing parents how to be 'better' at parenting. Children already have a teacher in school; they do not need another at home. And by whose criteria do we judge good parenting?

Although teachers often talk of wanting to involve the parents, we believe that parents *are* already involved in their children's education. By the time they take their children to nursery or to infant school, parents have already seen their children learn a large number of important things. They have learned to talk, to dress themselves, and to eat with a spoon and fork. They may also have learned to be rude, to get round their parents and to chew gum! Children will continue to learn, not only in school, but outside it; not only what they are taught, but what they pick up 'naturally'.

In many ways we can claim to have discovered a great deal about children's learning. In other ways, what we have learned is of little avail. We cannot predict with any degree of certainty what situations will advance learning, nor explain why one child learns something and another does not.

What we can do is to make links. We can help children to make connections between what they learn at home and what they learn at school. We can enable parents to link what children do in the classroom with their experiences at home. This book looks at how children learn. It considers the nature of the connections between learning at home and learning at school. It provides activities for parents to try out with their children, and a quiz which helps them to reflect upon what happened. It also explains the National Curriculum and the new arrangements for testing children.

Each chapter is divided as follows:

- some information, and some stories from our experience of parents and parenting;
- an activity to share with your child – these activities are suitable for children aged four to nine, although they may be adapted to suit children aged outside this range; and
- a quiz – this enables you to think about what took place as you shared the activity with your child. We also expect you to have a little fun doing them!

NB ***It is important to note that the scoring for the quiz has nothing to do with giving a score for either intelligence or performance. Its purpose is solely to provide a starting point from which to discuss the activity.***

The IMPACT project, out of which this book has been written, involves parents in their children's learning of maths through the use of weekly shared homework tasks. IMPACT – Maths with Parents And Children and Teachers – is currently running in approximately 500 schools around Britain. Over 20 000 children are taking home maths activities to share with their parents. In common with every IMPACT teacher, we are concerned to initiate conversations between home and school. Where these conversations lead, and the form which they take, is up to the parents, children and teachers themselves.

CHAPTER ONE

Parents into school go fine

Parents expect to play an important role in their children's education during the first three or four years of life. We parents do our best to ensure that our children have a stimulating and suitable environment, that they have other children with whom they can play, and that the advances they make in what they can do or say are noticed and encouraged.

When a child goes to school, whether to a nursery or a reception class, things alter drastically. Instead of feeling in control of the situation, many parents feel as if they are 'outsiders' to something. They see the teachers and staff controlling a great proportion of their child's experiences. Parents become observers rather than participants. From being players out on the field, they become spectators of the game!

SCHOOLS ARE SCARY!

One of the authors of this book has six children. When the eldest, Harry, now seventeen years old, was taken to school for the first time, there was a sense of loss, of abandoning a loved one. I was required to leave him, tearful, in the hands of his first teacher. In those days, parents were definitely not encouraged into the classroom. Indeed, we sometimes felt that there was an invisible alligator-filled trench across which parents were not allowed to cross!

Schools can seem quite strange and almost frightening places, not only to new and very young children, but also

to their unsuspecting parents. Some of us carry memories of being told off for running in the corridors, or for wearing too short a skirt. One of the authors recalls having his shoes removed by a teacher because they were 'pointed' rather then rounded at the toe. We may remember fierce teachers who seemed to possess an uncanny ability to see the thing that we felt most sensitive about and to point it out to the class. At worst, schools may not be places which we remember with love and affection but with a sense of failure and fear.

Nowadays, teachers are doing their best to make schools feel very different. Most schools welcome parents and are actively looking for ways in which to persuade them to come in and help in the classrooms, or at least to look at the children's work. Parents are encouraged to talk to the teachers about what is going on in the classroom, and to participate in their child's learning by helping at home.

NEW WAYS OF SEEING SCHOOLS

What has brought about this change in how schools see parents and how parents see schools? Over the last fifteen years we have come to see not only teachers but many other professionals in a slightly different light. When we take the baby along to the baby clinic, and have conversations with the health visitor or midwife we no longer expect to be 'told what to do'. At one time, the word of the doctor or midwife was law, and no patient felt there was a place for any questions. Nowadays, we expect to discuss the problem, and usually talk things through with the professional concerned. If we have a non-sleeping baby, the health visitor brings her professional knowledge and training into the conversation. Likewise, we bring our own special insight into our particular child and situation, our intuitive feelings and reactions. It is out of a conversation between parent and professional that (with some hope!) a solution is found, or at least a course of action agreed upon.

SHARED READING

In the late seventies and early eighties there were a number of initiatives in education which put the idea of a partnership between parents and teachers very much on the map. An increasing number of schools started to ask parents to read regularly with their children, and to fill out small reports about how the reading went. In this way, parents and teachers came to work much more closely together in an area of major importance to children's education.

One of the earliest of these 'shared reading' initiatives was PACT (Parents And Children and Teachers) associated with Alex Griffiths and Dorothy Hamilton. Children are encouraged to take a book home every evening and to share it with a parent or older sibling. There is a card or exercise book in which both parents and teachers write messages to each other concerning the child's reading. Other projects have imitated this, and many schools in England and Wales are now involved. Similar shared reading programmes include *CAPER* (Children And Parents Enjoying Reading) by Peter Branston and Mark Provis and *Paired Reading* (the Kirklees Paired Reading Project) by Keith Topping. See Appendix at the end of this book for further details of these.

The importance of the shared reading was not that it encouraged parents to read with their children, after all, most parents had been doing this anyway. The difference was that the contribution made by parents was 'official'; both looked for and valued by schools. Before shared reading, what parents did at home in terms of reading was ignored by the school. However, once PACT is set up, what the parents do at home is as important as what the teacher does at school. The parents, the teacher and the child are jointly engaged in a common purpose: reading a text.

When Harry was in the reception class in 1978, his teacher said to us that she hoped that we wouldn't read with him at home because they found it confused the child. Wilf started school two years ago, and as his teacher welcomed us she handed over a reading folder with Wilf's name on it, inside which was a book for comments. Wilf always comes home with his reading book and we have had many interesting conversations with his teacher about how things are going. Sometimes we will write a worried comment and his teacher will write back, or sometimes she has something to tell us, and we respond.

19.4.88

Chapters 1 and 2 The Disappearing Granny

Annie read this with some gusto and at some speed. Mistakes seemed to have more to do with care, or lack of it - Annie could deal with errors when re-reading at a slower pace. Annie like Banana Books. Very short words can present Annie with difficulty as long words — seems not to notice them often puts in ones of her own.

22.4.88

Good! There was a tendancy for Annie to rush, missing out bits and also finding it hard to get the general gist of the text. D

19/5/88

Annie read divinely! Had some trouble reading long sentences. Read them oddly. Brilliant Amazing, Ace and Generally wicked

Harry

Yeah, Sure Harry!
(p.s good work!)

However, even if the teacher and the parents are working together in this way, it does not mean that learning to read is *always* enjoyable or problem free for the child. Wilf loves being read to, but is very reluctant to read himself. He has four older brothers and sisters who will happily do things for him, and we sometimes joke that, like the Emperor of China, he will still be being dressed at sixteen! However, if his non-reading became a real difficulty, we and the teachers would have a background of conversations on which to base any discussion about which strategies to adopt.

Reading at home is very demanding, and parents can start to wonder if they are not being required to do the teacher's job for them! Especially if the child is sometimes reluctant, a parent may feel that work is work and should be done in school and home is for relaxing and playing. Or course, we do not want children to see reading as 'work', even though learning to read can be quite hard. We want children to like books, and to see them as the great source of enjoyment which they are. If small children are taught to read out of a sense of duty or for rewards, such as sweets or money, then they are very unlikely to read from choice when they are older and have outgrown sweets! Although we are unlikely to lose a desire for money it will be rare to find someone being paid to enjoy books. And, in any case, there is little reason to suppose that rewarding with sweets or money will do anything other than harm in the long run.

DON'T TEACHERS TEACH ANY MORE?

A parent in Wales has summed up these concerns by saying, 'Miners mine, nurses nurse; don't teachers teach anymore?' The teachers answered by describing how, when we have been in hospital, we are encouraged to come home and look after ourselves. The nurses will suggest that we take things easy, perhaps we have some medicine, and we generally continue to 'nurse ourselves' at home for a while. In this way, the nurse and the patient are partners. They collaborate to make the patient better. Neither one can do as well on their own, but together they can be pretty effective.

The same is true in teaching. The teacher does her bit, and the parent does likewise. We hope the child is motivated to do her bit as well! As we talk about how things are going, we build up a real partnership to the benefit of the child's learning. There is now a great deal of evidence that parental involvement can assist children's success at school. If we, as parents, want our children to do well, we have to involve ourselves in the *details* of their education. What counts is being prepared to listen to our own children read, night after night, and to share books and conversations with them.

SHARED MATHS

The IMPACT project, out of which this book arose, was another attempt to involve parents in their children's education. This time we were concerned not with reading, but with maths.

Most of us do not have wonderful memories of maths at school. For many people, maths was boring and bewildering, a jumble of procedures and difficult ideas which we never quite managed to come to grips with. Mathematicians have the reputation, quite erroneously, of being 'clever'. Actually, mathematicians in our experience, are no more and no less likely to be highly intelligent than anyone else. They are simply folk who have acquired a particular set of skills. We will discuss how maths is perceived, and what our attitudes and assumptions are concerning it, later in the book in Chapter 5.

Through IMPACT, many thousands of parents have come to be involved in their children's learning of maths. They share weekly or fortnightly maths activities with their children, and then comment on how these went. This sounds very alarming, but in fact the parents tell us that they mostly have a lot of fun.

One small child, Sally, brought home an activity in which she was asked to go through the store cupboard and find things which would roll, and things which wouldn't roll but would slide. She had to sort them into two piles, and draw one of each. Her mother told us that Sally insisted on finding every single thing in the kitchen which would roll or slide, including the salt cellar, which rolled beautifully. But, she lamented, it was not Sally who had to hoover the floor afterwards!

Another child, Amit, had to measure the volume of his body by lying in the bath, and then seeing how much the water level dropped when he got out. He was also asked to measure someone else in the family, and his mother complained that she had the greatest difficulty in preventing him from drowning the baby!

Schools which are a part of IMPACT, and there are over 500 of them, find that the main benefit to children's learning comes from the fact that the children have to talk about all the maths that they are doing. They learn something at school, and then take it home and discuss it with their family. This is quite different from the more traditional sort of conversation about school which takes place at home between parent and child. Such conversations are two a penny in our house:

'What did you do at school today, Fred?' Fred (aged 7), 'Nothing.'

'Well, you *must* have done *something*. What did you do?'
'We had pink custard for lunch.'
'Well, *apart* from what you had for lunch, didn't you do anything interesting?'
'I had a fight with Robert in the playground. . . '

Fred is a torturer's nightmare. Getting information out of him is like trying to get blood from a stone.

However, when Fred comes in and tells us that he has to measure the head circumference of everyone in the family, he talks nineteen to the dozen. From Fred's point of view, the question, 'What did you do at school today?' is a boring question. It is like, 'Did you have a nice day at the office, dear?' But when he comes in with a task to do in which he is in charge, and has to explain to the rest of us what has to be done, and how, then the situation is quite different.

PARENTS PLAY A PART TOO

Schemes like PACT, CAPER and IMPACT are important because they are an indication of how things have changed in terms of the role which parents are expected to play in their child's schooling. Once the child enters the school, parents are no longer required to hand over control to 'experts' who know better. Parents have expertise as far as their own child goes; teachers have professional expertise. It is when we put these two things together and collaborate that we can expect the best results for the child's experience of school in particular and their education in general.

ACTIVITY AND QUIZ

Each chapter of this book has an activity for you to share with your child. As you do the activity, notice how it goes. Try to make a note of the parts your child particularly enjoys and the bits she has difficulty with. Does your child talk a lot, and appear to be taking the lead in the conversation? After sharing the activity, do the quiz below it.

ACTIVITY

Choose a short book which your child likes. Read it together. If your child can read, encourage her to read some parts on her own. Then talk about the book. You could discuss the characters in the story, where the story takes place, whether it is funny or sad or if it is exciting. Look at the pictures, and ask your child if they fit in with the story.

Concentrate upon the numbering of the pages. Ask what happens on page one, on the third page and so on . . . Does your child understand 'fourth' and 'fifth', as well as four and five? Can she find her initial on each page? How many times does it occur?

For older children ask them to guess how many words there are on a page, or what the common words are in the story, or to find the unusual words.

Now answer the questions in the quiz.

QUIZ

1 Did your child enjoy reading the book with you?

(a) A great deal.

(b) Quite a bit.

(c) Not very much.

(d) Not at all.

2 Did you argue over who would read which parts?

(a) Your child didn't want to read.

(b) You didn't want your child to read.

(c) You both wanted to read the same bits.

(d) You didn't argue at all.

3 Did your child enjoy the conversation after you had finished the book?

(a) Very much indeed.

(b) Quite a lot.

(c) A bit.

(d) Not at all.

4 During the conversation who did most of the talking?

(a) Your child.

(b) You.

(c) It was equally balanced.

(d) Someone else, e.g. a brother or sister.

5 What was the nature of the conversation?

(a) Mostly question and answer with you asking the questions.

(b) Mostly question and answer with your child asking the questions.

(c) A lively discussion.

(d) Short and boring.

6 When looking at the number aspects of the activity, how did your child get on?

(a) Answered questions correctly.

(b) Answered questions incorrectly.

(c) Avoided answering altogether.

(d) You didn't notice because you were too busy talking?

7 How much would you say that doing this activity helped your child?

(a) Quite a lot.

(b) A fair amount.

(c) A bit.

(d) Not at all.

SCORING YOUR QUIZ

	(a)	(b)	(c)	(d)
1	8	6	2	0
2	0	3	5	4
3	8	6	3	0
4	8	1	5	2
5	1	4	5	2
6	3	3	1	6
7	5	4	3	1

Under 15

You may not yet be convinced of the value of your own role in helping your child to read and enjoy books. Remember that the home and your attitude to books are probably the most important factors in developing your child's ability to read and to take pleasure in reading. Children do as we do (unfortunately!), not as we say! How much we enjoy books ourselves, how often we choose to read, and whether we are seen to buy and treasure books, are all indications to the child of our attitudes to reading, and of the importance it really has in our lives. Similarly, parents are influential in developing a positive attitude to maths in a child. The maths that we do as we go about our normal routines may not look or feel much like the maths we did at school; but it is crucial in helping children to acquire mathematical skills and apply these in everyday life. Do not be tempted to undervalue the importance of your own role. Parents do not need to 'teach' their children to read or do maths, but they can *enable* children to do these things with confidence. In order to do this, we do not need to be brilliant mathematicians or expert readers. Enthusiasm and time are all that are required

16-31

You and your child do seem to enjoy reading together and discussing the points raised. You see the importance of your parental role in assisting your child's development by sharing books and talking about them. However, it may be that it is sometimes difficult for your child to lead the conversation. Questions and answers are not always a good format for a real discussion and it is important that your child is encouraged to put forward her own questions and take the conversation in an unexpected direction. Where maths goes, it is possible that you feel less confident in this area than you do with reading. But remember, the importance of the parents' role in a child's education does *not* depend upon their ability to teach or even to understand the maths that their child is learning. Parents do not need to 'teach' their children to read or do maths, but they can *enable* children to do these things with confidence. In order to do this, we do not need to be brilliant mathematicians or expert readers. Enthusiasm and time are all that are required.

Over 32

You and your child have clearly shared books and discussed them on many occasions. You are used to having conversations about what you read together and in taking time over each aspect that interests you. But it may be important that you try to allow your child her own opinions and do not influence her too strongly. As parents we are sometimes prone to let our feelings run away with us. We find it a shock when our children dislike something we regard as excellent, or express delight in something we regard as inferior or in poor taste. But children must be their own persons, and we can only assist them to form judgements if we listen as well as tell, hear as well as explain. Where maths is concerned, it is equally important that children come to discover things for themselves, rather than always being told how things are. Maths is as creative and open-ended a subject as any other. It is a great mistake to believe that it is all about getting the right answer. Children need to be encouraged to *think* mathemathically rather than follow given rules. Parents do not need to 'teach' their children to read or to do maths, but they can *enable* children to do these things with confidence. In order to do this, we do not need to be brilliant mathematicians or expert readers. Enthusiasm and time are all that are required.

POINT TO REMEMBER

Parents have a role to play in their children's education. Schools have been increasingly recognising the crucial importance of this role over the last ten years, and parents are, for the most part, encouraged to come into the school and to take an active part in the children's learning. We should no longer see schools as fearful institutions or teachers as alien beings, automatically 'expert' in knowing what is best for our children.

There are now many ways in which parents can be asked by teachers to collaborate in assisting the children's learning. We can read with our children on a regular basis and let the teacher know how they are getting on. We can share maths activities either as a part of our normal routines as they arise – counting out the change, watching out for the time when *Neighbours* starts, and so on – or when the teacher sends something home from school. We can all keep talking – children with parents, parents with children, teachers to parents and parents to teachers!

Partnership between parents and teachers is the most effective way of improving children's learning. We have all got everything to gain and nothing to lose by collaboration. At the end of the day, it is always much more fun and more rewarding to work together than separately. And a problem shared is often a problem halved. So we start as we mean to go on, by working with the school and talking to the teachers. Not such a bad fate after all!

CHAPTER TWO

Children learning

When children are little and we have them at home, we take it for granted that they are learning all the time. We sometimes describe such learning as 'natural'. 'Oh, he seems to have picked it up naturally', we might say when Fred has mastered the art of putting on his pyjamas or peeling a tangerine. This, *in our own minds,* makes a distinction between skills which the children do pick up naturally and other skills, such as reading or writing, which we feel they have to be taught.

SMALL CHILDREN AS LEARNERS

In our house, where we have six children, we often joke that the children seem to acquire, without any problem, 'bad' or useless skills such as blowing bubbles with bubble-gum; yet they have the utmost difficulty in learning how to do perfectly simple but useful things such as closing a door quietly, or washing up a plate and mug!

By the time our children go to school, we have already seen them learn an enormous amount. They have learned how to feed themselves – well, more or less! From a baby's first tentative and messy attempts with spoonfulls of mushy porridge, through to the five-year-old's competency with a knife and fork, there is a great deal of imitation, practice and improvement.

Children have also learned how to dress themselves. A baby who starts to stretch his arm into a jersey, will gradually realise that he can pull his jersey over his own head. We have found that

many children seem to find it easier to undress than to dress. But, by persevering, they all eventually master the art of dressing. Indeed, when we consider how hard some adult clothes are to get into, we can see just how competent we all become.

Sometimes we actively teach children a particular skill. Crossing the road is not something which we would want the child to learn by trial and error. We have set procedures, 'Look right, look left, look right again', and we give instructions, 'Stop, look, listen.' We help children to learn, for example, by making them aware of time and place, 'Always wait until you can see that the road is clear . . . This is a good place to cross.'

And of course, by the time the child is five, she has already acquired the most complex and amazing skills. She has learned how to talk. She can express herself and make needs known competently through the spoken word. Children as young as eighteen months can often string words together to make sense, give instructions and express a desire. Our youngest child, Matthew, aged twenty-two months, came into the room in a great state of agitation and upset, gathered his wits together, and said slowly and deliberately, 'Annie (his older sister) hit me'. Annie, also in the room, looked suitably guilty. She realised that she was no longer safe – Matthew had learned to tell tales!

LEARNING AT SCHOOL

However, it is when children start school that what we think of as 'serious' learning takes place. When we have asked parents to describe the ideal child in an ideal learning situation at school, we have found that they tend to talk of silent classrooms, children sitting at desks with books, paper and pencils. Perhaps this has rather more to do with how some of us remember school than with what we have seen of our own children's learning.

But we should perhaps contrast this with what we remember about how we learned ourselves. Many of us would spend an unhappy maths lesson, confused and puzzled in a quiet classroom, listening to a teacher who seemed to go faster all the time, and who never made any sense. We did our best to avoid answering questions or having to talk about what we were doing. Most of the time, we didn't actually know what we were doing, much less why we were doing it! But, come the bus ride home, how many of us asked questions and did our maths homework together with our friends? Lively arguments would take place about whether that particular figure should be a two or a two squared, or what the correct area of a triangle was. Most of the learning and understanding of maths did not occur in our silent classroom, it took place on the bus when Jane showed us how this worked, or Patrick explained that.

When we ask parents to remember something that they have just learned, we get a different view of learning again. Very often, the learning involves another person, or a conversation. Perhaps we had to learn how to programme the video. (Take the ten-year-old daughter who had to explain patiently to her less technically minded parent which buttons to press and in what order.) Perhaps there was a new word-processor in the office. As often as not, three or four people help each other to make sense of an apparently incomprehensible booklet of instructions.

TALKING AT HOME

Children need to talk as they learn, as indeed do most adults. We need to explain things to ourselves, to put the problem into our own words. We need to make information our own by rewording it for ourselves. When we have observed children learning at home, we have seen how much they, rather than the adult, are the 'leaders' in conversations. A typical piece of chatter in the home is likely to consist of the child taking the parent through a conversation with a topic of their own choosing. Here is the dialogue of a three-year-old, talking to his mother who is washing up.

'I'm being Batman . . . Batman has a cloak . . . Can I have a cloak? I need a cloak? Where's a cloak for me?'

'Your cloak is upstairs, in your bedroom . . Go and get it . . . It's by your bed.'
'I can get it . . . I can go upstairs . . . Mummy put it on . . . I bring my cloak to Mummy . . . Batman has a cloak . . . '

Often children will work out how a problem is to be solved (in this case, the acquisition of Batman's vital outer garment) through the course of a conversation with another person. They lead the conversation, and by active steps they take it in the direction in which they want it to go.

LEARNING WHERE?

Psychologists, looking at maths, have found that what children do with maths problems, that is which ones they can solve and which ones they can't, is greatly affected by the situation in which the problem arises. Children, like adults, find it much easier to solve problems, or at least to work out *how* to solve them, if they occur naturally as a part of what they are doing, rather than as an isolated part of something like a maths lesson. (Although it should be said that some people are at home in school-maths but cannot do it anywhere else.)

At home, we often have to ask children to use specifically mathematical skills. We say 'Can you look in the biscuit tin and see how many chocolate biscuits your greedy brother has left for the rest of us?' This is a genuine request for information. We do not know how many biscuits there are. The child is to find out and tell us. Of course, they may decide to tell us the wrong answer, or to lie! In the classroom, similar questions are actually rather different. The child had threaded beads on to a string and the teacher asks, 'Well, how many beads have you threaded on to your necklace there?' The child knows that this is *not* a request for information, and that the teacher *knows* how many beads there are on the string. They are aware that this question is a 'testing' question; it is asking, 'Do *you* know how many beads there are . . . Can you work it out?' Although the two questions sound similar, they are in fact quite different.

Furthermore, maths problems, like any others, are not the same problems from one situation to another. They may look the same superficially, but any observation of how problems are successfully solved in real life shows us that the problems themselves, and the ways in which we solve them, are dependent upon the situation in which they arise.

ACTIVITY

Try out this activity with your child. Watch carefully what happens – how you and your child approach the task and how much learning you feel takes place. After you have done the activity together, complete the quiz. Then read on!

This activity is suitable for children aged four to eight. Younger or older children may also get something out of it but you may need to be a little creative in adapting it.

You will need: Approximately fifteen spoons (unless you are very tall and the spoons are very small, in which case you will need more!) A space in which to lie down and be measured.

1 Tell your child you are going to let her measure you with spoons! Five-year-olds we know thought this was a hilarious idea!

2 Hand her the spoons, and lie down on the floor. Just as she is about to start, ask her how many spoons she thinks it will take.

3 As she starts laying the spoons beside you, you may need to discuss whether the spoons touch or overlap. You may also need to talk about where she starts.

4 When she has got halfway, ask her to guess again how many spoons she thinks she is going to have to use. This gives her a chance to revise her estimate in the light of what she has seen so far.

5 When she finishes, ask her how wrong, or how right, she was. An older child may be encouraged to work out the difference (in number of spoons) between their guess and the final number.

6 Now get up (whew!), and tell her that it is your turn to measure her in spoons. Ask her how many she thinks it will take?

7 Now measure her (lying down!) counting the spoons as you go.

8 Perhaps you can then measure someone or something else in the room. (Wilf went on measuring for hours. Even the cat got measured!)

QUIZ

1 How much did your child enjoy the activity?

(a) A great deal.

(b) Quite a bit.

(c) A small amount.

(d) Not at all.

2 Which part did she enjoy the most?

(a) The laying down of the spoons.

(b) The counting.

(c) The guessing.

(d) Ordering you around, getting you to lie down on the floor, and so on.

3 Did your child have difficulty with any of the following?

(a) Laying the spoons end to end.

(b) Counting.

(c) Coming up with a reasonable guess.

(d) No particular part.

4 How much did you feel your child learned?

(a) A great deal.

(b) A bit about one aspect.

(c) Not very much.

(d) She got confused.

5 From which part of the activity do you feel your child gained most?

(a) The practical task of actually having to lay things end-to-end and measure.

(b) Practising counting.

(c) Trying to guess accurately.

(d) Having your undivided attention throughout the whole thing.

6 Did your child chatter throughout the activity?

(a) A great deal.

(b) Not much.

(c) Only in reply to your questions.

(d) Not at all.

7 What parts did your child talk about most?

(a) The practical parts of the activity.

(b) The counting parts.

(c) Having to guess.

(d) The whole activity.

SCORING YOUR QUIZ

	(a)	*(b)*	*(c)*	*(d)*
1	8	5	2	0
2	3	1	2	4
3	1	3	2	0
4	8	5	2	0
5	3	2	4	5
6	8	4	3	0
7	4	1	2	5

Under 15

It is likely that this activity was either much too easy or too hard for your child since she did not seem to get a great deal out of it. Sometimes children are not in the mood to do a particular type of task, or sometimes the task itself just does not suit the child. After all, you cannot please all of the people all of the time! But it is important to make sure that your child does get the chance to discuss things, and that she does talk to you about activities as she does them. Children benefit immensely from working things out and by talking to an adult as they do them. This is true whether they are learning how to do something mundane like washing the dishes, or a piece of formal maths like a subtraction sum.

16–26

There were obviously some parts of this activity which appealed to your child, and others where she was less certain. Perhaps she lacks confidence in particular areas, or had a bit of trouble with one part. However, other aspects did go well and there was some discussion and consequent learning. Often children will learn more from an activity which they do as a part of what is going on anyway (such as laying the table or sorting the washing) than they do from an activity which is set up specially as this one was! The more they can talk through what they are doing, as they are doing it, in their own way, the more they are likely to learn.

Over 27

This activity obviously stimulated a lot of discussion and fun. Possibly, your child really liked having your undivided attention, and took the opportunity to talk through each aspect as she went along. If you have both enjoyed this, then it could be that you could try some of the other activities in Chapter 6 and see how they go. Perhaps your child is ready to try out a number of new skills at the moment and the more opportunities for talking about what she is doing, the better. It may be that this activity also linked with what she is doing at school or in another situation. It is always nice for children, just as it is for adults, to be able to make links between one thing they are doing, and another.

POINTS TO REMEMBER

Children, like the rest of us, are working things out as they go along.

First, they have to put the problem into their own words. This enables them to work out exactly what the problem involves. They can do this by talking out loud, by 'talking to themselves' in silence, or by involving others in the conversation.

Second, they will try out various methods of solving the problem. This may involve them in looking for help or in adapting their own methods as they see what works and what doesn't.

As children, or adults, are solving problems, part of the process may involve acquiring a new skill. To do this, help will sometimes be needed. Such help can involve:

- allowing children to copy or imitate a more competent person (e.g. showing them how to roll out pastry);
- giving them instructions (e.g. telling them how to walk to Granny's);
- physically assisting them (e.g. holding the back of the bike as they learn to ride it); or
- talking them through a process or procedure (e.g. helping them to tie shoelaces).

But of course, help is not *always* needed, and nothing is more infuriating to children than being helped when they want to try something on their own. 'Do it *self!*', Matthew yells in our house, as one of his older brothers or sisters insists on trying to help him as he struggles inexpertly to pour his own milk on to his cornflakes. And unless we can put up with the mess, and the fact that certain things won't be done as well, the children will not learn. They have to walk around with their shoelaces badly tied for a while, before they get good at it. The alternative of retying them is upsetting for the child in that it devalues her efforts and shows up her lack of competence.

But talk is always helpful, and one of the most important aspects of learning is the ability to organise the conversation by which things are made clear to ourselves. Learning is rarely silent, and even when it is, there is talk going on inside our heads. Although we may spend a lot of time telling children to go away and keep quiet, it is just as well that they rarely take much notice!

CHAPTER THREE

The National Curriculum

No parent who has come into contact with schools can have failed to notice that we now have a National Curriculum. However, it may be less than clear what this actually means in practice. Many parents have read or heard conflicting information such as . . . perhaps the National Curriculum will mean that children will be tested a great deal more than they are now . . . or it will set them learning things by rote . . . or they will have to stop working in groups at tables and go back to sitting in rows behind desks . . . perhaps they will no longer be allowed to talk in class. . .

So, what does the National Curriculum actually mean? What changes will it make to how schools are run and to how teachers teach?

THE CURRICULUM CONTENT

The most obvious difference made by the National Curriculum concerns what children are taught. Since the 1988 Education Reform Act, the law has laid down all those things in each subject which teachers have a duty to cover during a child's education. Thus, in mathematics, we are told that children should learn to 'count, read, write and order the numbers to 10' in their first year or so at school.

In order to describe what children should be taught, the Education Reform Act had to take into account the following:

- Children learn different things at different times. One child may have learned to count by the time she

Knowledge, skills, understanding and use and number, algebra and measures (ATs 1–8).

Attainment Target 2: Number

Pupils should understand number and number notation.

LEVEL	STATEMENTS OF ATTAINMENT	EXAMPLE
	Pupils should:	
1	• **count, read, write and order numbers to at least 10; know that the size of a set is given by the last number in the count.**	
	• **understand the conservation of number.**	*Know that if a set of 8 pencils is counted, the answer is always the same however they are arranged.*
2	• **read, write and order numbers to at least 100; use the knowledge that the tens-digit indicates the number of tens.**	*Know that 37 means 3 tens and 7 units; know that three 10p coins and four 1p coins give 34p.*
	• **understand the meaning of a 'half' and 'a quarter'.**	*Find a quarter of a piece of string; know that half of 8 is 4.*
3	• **read, write and order numbers to at least 1000; use the knowledge that the position of a digit indicates its value.**	*Know that 'four hundred and two' is written 402 and why neither 42 nor 4002 is correct.*
	• **use decimal notation as the conventional way of recording in money.**	*Know that three £1 coins plus six 1p coins is written as £3.06, and that 3·6 on a calculator means £3·60 in the context of money.*
	• **appreciate the meaning of negative whole numbers in familiar contexts.**	*Read a temperature scale; understand a negative output on a calculator.*
4	• **read, write and order whole numbers.**	
	• **understand the effect of multiplying a whole number by 10 or 100.**	*Explain why the cost of 10 objects costing £23 each is £230.*
	• **use, with understanding, decimal notation; to two decimal places in the context of measurement.**	*Read scales marked in hundredths and numbered in tenths (1·89 m).*
	• **recognise and understand simple everyday fractions.**	*Estimate ⅓ of a pint of milk or ¾ of the length of a piece of wood.*
	• **recognise and understand simple percentages.**	*Know that 7 books out of a total of 100 books represents 7%.*
	• **understand and use the relationship between place values in whole numbers.**	*Know that 5000 is 5 thousands or 50 hundreds or 500 tens or 5000 ones.*

Page extract from Mathematics in the National Curriculum (*reproduced with the permission of the Controller of Her Majesty's Stationery Office*) comes to school, but may have no clue about the alphabet or reading. Another may be reading quite well at five, but perhaps cannot tie up her shoelaces, recognise a square or hop on one leg.

- Some children learn slowly and some learn quickly. It may take one child *ages* to learn to count to twenty, but she may recognise words without any problem. Something which takes one child an afternoon to get hold of might take another child three weeks!
- How slowly or how fast children learn something does not necessarily tell us anything about how intelligent they are. It may be that they are interested in that topic, or that they find a particular thing especially easy or difficult.
- Teachers do come to know the children they teach and often develop quite a reliable sense of what they can and can't do. Any testing of the children is likely to be much more effective and helpful if it takes the teacher's personal knowledge into account.
- Learning quite often happens in 'spurts'! A child will plod along not seeming to learn much for a while, and then all of a sudden, she will change so fast that we almost can't believe it's the same child. It is often the same with physical development. Children stay the same size for ages and then suddenly they grow three sizes at once.
- The band of what it is normal for a child to know, what skills we can reasonably expect them to have, at any specific age, is very broad. It is quite normal for a child to be reading at five, or not reading at all until seven. It is absolutely normal for a child to come into school counting to 100, and for another child not to recognise any of the numbers up to five. This does not seem so bizarre if we remember that the normal birth weight for a baby in Britain today can vary between five and ten pounds. A baby of ten pounds is on the heavy side but not abnormal, and a baby of five pounds is on the light side. Children vary in a similar way in their development and what is normal for one child is advanced for another.

The National Curriculum maps out for teachers the ground that must be covered in terms of what maths, English and science (and the other subjects) should be taught. But it does not spell out *when* each child must do each of these topics, or *how* the teacher must teach.

PARENTS AND TEACHERS

In certain ways, being a teacher is a bit like being a parent. We can all recognise good parenting, even if we ourselves can't always achieve it! 'Mary makes a good Mum,' we may comment, and others may agree with us. But it is much harder to spell out precisely the necessary qualities. We might claim that patience seems important, but Mary may not be a particularly patient person, although she is universally recognised as a good mother. A sense of humour is surely essential, and good organisational skills or efficiency certainly help. But we all know people who don't seem to possess these qualities in especially large measures, and yet who seem to make exceptional parents.

The situation is even more complicated when we realise that one person's way of parenting, which may work really well for them, may be totally unsuitable if another person were to try it. My methods of controlling, organising and repsonding to my children may be quite unlike yours. What is excellent practice for Jemima could be a disaster zone for Mary, and vice versa.

Teaching is very similar. We can all recognise the excellent or gifted teacher. We can see when a particular teacher is doing a really good job. But if we try to list the things which a person must do in order to be a good teacher, we find it almost impossible. Some teachers run quiet and orderly classrooms. With others, the children flourish in the lively bustle of a stimulating environment. All teachers need to plan, but some do so in an almost computer-like and precise fashion, while others prefer a loose and flexible system.

If we were to force all teachers to teach in a particular way by law, we would stifle some and destroy others. We certainly would not get the best out of our teachers. This is because we recognise that there is no one correct or right way to teach. Teaching is not that sort of skill.

We cannot claim to be wonderful parents. When you drop the Marmite pot, upset the tea over the floor, and shout at the toddler, your seventeen-year-old son asks you sarcastically, 'Going for "mother-of-the-year" award again are we, Mum?' But if a law were passed which told us *exactly how* we were to mother or father our children and what methods we must use to bring them up, we very much doubt if this would improve matters at all! There are as many ways of parenting as there are parents, and there are possibly as many ways of teaching well as there are teachers.

WHAT HAS TO BE TAUGHT

The National Curriculum provides a framework within which teachers now have to work. They are given the content of the curriculum, and now know what skills or facts children have to learn at each stage of their school career. Once we have read and understood the National Curriculum, teachers can then set about delivering it in their own way.

What is in the National Curriculum has not come as a surprise to anyone involved in education. Those things which have gone in under the headings of maths, science and English, as well as into the other subjects, are still things which we have been teaching for some time. What caused the raising of a few eyebrows, was firstly how the National Curriculum was arranged, and secondly what got in under each subject.

THE ARRANGEMENT OF THE NATIONAL CURRICULUM

There are three Core subjects – maths, English and science – and seven Foundation subjects – history, geography, physical education, design and technology, art, music, and a modern language to be taught from eleven years upwards.

Each subject tells us what the children need to know, and this is described in *ten* levels of Attainment. This means that we can picture each subject as containing a series of ladders up which children have to climb.

Children will climb these ladders as fast or as slowly as they can. But they are expected to progress at a rate of approximately one level in every two years of schooling. For guidance:

- the average seven-year-old is expected to be on Level 2;
- the average eleven-year-old is expected to be on Level 4;
- the average fourteen-year-old is expected to be on Level 6.

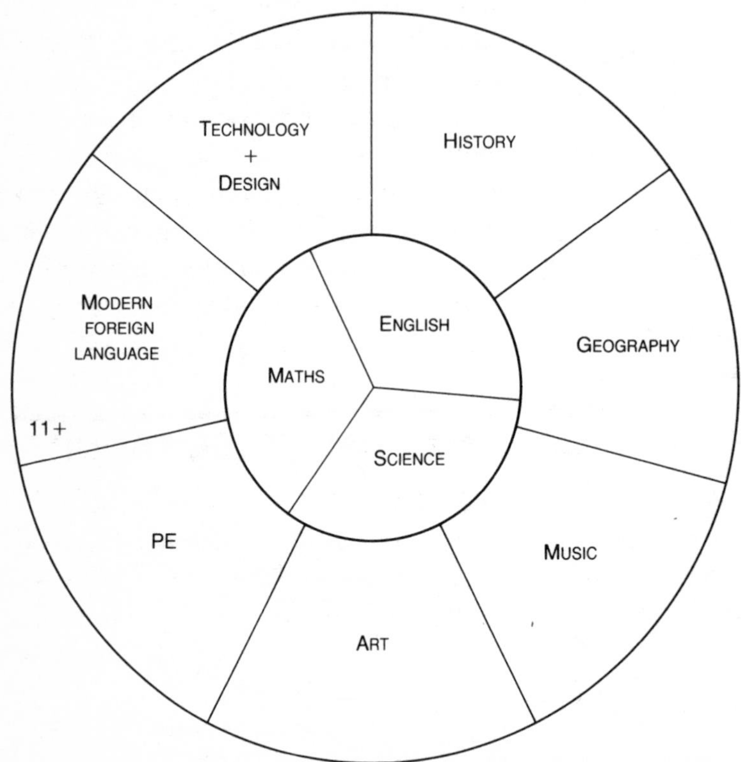

Core subjects:
English, maths, science,

Other Foundation subjects:
PE, art, music, geography, history, technology & design modern foreign language.

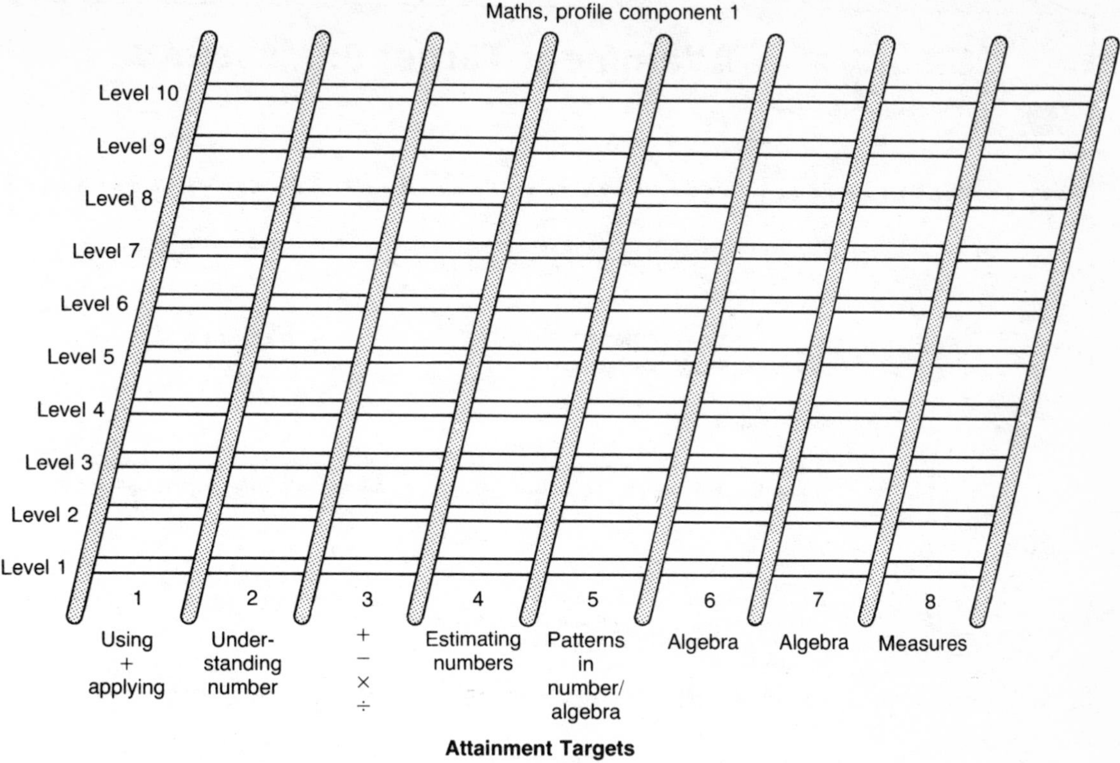

ATTAINMENT TARGETS

In addition to being arranged in ten levels, every subject is described in a series of Attainment Targets. These are, roughly speaking, areas within the subjects. For example, in maths, one of the Attainment Targets is 'Understanding number; another is 'Measures'; and so on.

In the core subjects there are thirty-six Attainment Targets. There are seventeen in science, fourteen in maths and five in English. This does *not* mean that English is a less important subject than science; it simply reflects the way that the experts in that field chose to divide up their subject.

NO 'BACK TO BASICS'

Those who wanted to see the National Curriculum present us with a complete change in *what* is taught have been sorely disappointed. None of the core subjects leaves out those topics or processes which have been to the fore in teaching maths, English and science over the last ten, or even fifteen years. So, in maths we find subjects like topology, handling data, probability and so on. These are hardly subjects which many of us adults associate with all the maths we knew and loved when we were at school. In other words, the 'new maths' is firmly in place, and we may as well come to terms with the fact that these changes are here to stay.

Knowledge, skills, understanding and use and number, algebra and measures (ATs 1–8).

Attainment Target 8: Measures

Pupils should estimate and measure quantities, and appreciate the approximate nature of measurement.

LEVEL	STATEMENTS OF ATTAINMENT	EXAMPLE
	Pupils should:	
1	• compare and order objects without measuring, and use appropriate language.	*Use language such as: long, longer than, longest; tall, taller than, tallest; heavy, light; before, after; hot, cold.*
2	• use non-standard measures in length, area, volume, capacity, 'weight' and time to compare objects and recognise the need to use standard units.	*Use handspans, strips of paper, conkers, etc. as measures.*
	• know how to use coins in simple contexts.	*Handle money – shopping activities in the classroom.*
	• know the most commonly used units in length, capacity, 'weight' and time, and what they are used for.	*Suggest things which are commonly measured in metres, miles, litres, pints, pounds, seconds, minutes, hours, etc.*
3	• use a wider range of metric units.	*Use centimetre, kilometre, gram.*
	• choose and use appropriate units and instruments in a variety of situations, interpreting numbers on a range of measuring instruments.	*Use an appropriate tape/ruler to compare lengths that cannot be put side by side.* *Read digital clocks correctly and analogue clocks to the nearest labelled division.* *Read a speedometer on a car or bicycle correctly.*
	• make estimates based on familiar units.	*Estimate the height of a door in metres, the capacity of a bottle in litres, or a period of time.*
4	• understand the relationship between units.	*Use two units such as millilitres and litres to measure the capacity of the same jug.*
	• find areas by counting squares, and volumes by counting cubes, using whole numbers.	*Find the approximate area of a leaf; work out the approximate volume of a small box.*
	• make sensible estimates of a range of measures in relation to everyday objects or events.	*Estimate the length of a car, the capacity of a teacup, the 'weight' of a school bag.* *Use timetables to anticipate time of arrival.* *Estimate the time taken to complete a task.*

21

Page extract from Mathematics in the National Curriculum *(reproduced with the permission of the Controller of Her Majesty's Stationery Office)*

ALL CHANGE

The National Curriculum represents a major change in the British education system. For the first time ever we have it laid down exactly what things, in each subject, all state schools have to teach. Parents are entitled to be told what their children are going to be working on at any stage in their school career. They are also entitled to hear how their child is progressing through the ten levels of attainment in each part of each subject.

Teachers have, by law, to deliver the National Curriculum. They have to produce written and detailed plans in advance as to what work the children will actually be doing. They also have to produce and maintain careful records as to how each child is progressing on every single attainment target in each subject.

There are those teachers who complain that they did not choose to be a teacher in order to push paper around. There are those parents who comment that they would rather see a happy teacher with happy children than a detailed plan of the Scheme of Work for their child. But the Education Reform Act is here to stay and education must reshape itself into the mould provided.

ACTIVITY

You will need eight or ten smallish objects on a tray. For example, you might have an egg-cup, some keys, a glass of water, a bar of chocolate, a spoon, a jar of jam, a candle, and a box of matches.

Ask your child to look at the tray carefully for a short period of time, say fifteen seconds. Then, blindfold her and turn her around three times. Meanwhile, you remove one of the items from the tray. Now unblindfold your child and see if she can tell you which object is missing?

There are various things you can do to make the game either harder or easier: Try:

- reducing the number of objects on the tray;
- talking about each thing before you blindfold your child;
- turning your child round, when blindfold, more than three times;
- putting more things on the tray;
- adding to the tray rather than taking something off; or
- replacing an object rather than removing it.

You can try this game on adults too! Children love to try to catch a grown-up out, and it is not as easy as it looks.

QUIZ

1 Did you find the task?

(a) A lot harder than expected.

(b) A bit harder than expected.

(c) About the same as expected.

(d) A bit easier than expected.

2 Which of the following helped your child?

(a) Giving her longer to look at the tray.

(b) Talking about the things on the tray.

(c) Twirling your child round and round fewer times.

(d) Putting fewer things on the tray.

3 Did your child enjoy the game?

(a) A lot.

(b) Quite a bit.

(c) Only at first.

(d) Not at all.

4 Could you have predicted in advance how your child would get on?

(a) Yes, totally.

(b) Not really.

(c) Not at all.

5 Do you think that if someone else, other than you, had been doing the activity with your child, she would have performed differently?

(a) She might have done better.

(b) She would not have done so well.

(c) It makes no difference, it's the task that counts, not who does it.

(d) It would depend who the other person was.

6 Which of the following would you say that this activity depended upon?

(a) Having a good memory.

(b) Being interested in the things on the tray.

(c) Having the will to succeed.

(d) A mixture of all the above.

7 Which of the following did your child benefit from?

(a) The conversation and attention from you.

(b) The memory practice iinvolved.

(c) Being asked to concentrate on her own.

(d) Nothing at all.

SCORING YOUR QUIZ

	(a)	(b)	(c)	(d)
1	8	3	0	2
2	4	6	5	2
3	5	3	2	1
4	1	3	6	
5	4	2	0	5
6	2	4	1	6
7	6	2	3	1

Under 15
You are concerned that your child does well in any situation, especially one in which you feel she might be being judged or tested. You try to help by giving advice or telling her a better way to approach the task. Perhaps because you think quite quickly yourself, you have difficulty in slowing down or imagining yourself in a child's shoes. It is important to remember that even the most caring parent cannot do the thinking and learning *for* the child. Children have to develop their own thoughts and think through their own ideas. The adult may be quite clear as to what should happen in a particular activity, and the best way of achieving it, but the child may find other things to be hard. She may have difficulties we could not have predicted. Things which seem irrelevant to us turn out to be extremely important in helping or in hindering a child. Given all this, the extent to which we can plan a child's learning in advance must be open to question. If learning were simply a matter of listening and being told, it would be easy. But setting up suitable learning experiences, knowing when to interfere and when to let a child struggle alone, make teaching a great deal more like parenting than like programming a computer.

16–30
You are keen to help your child to succeed in any task she is undertaking. You will offer help and make suggestions but you are also prepared to listen to her ideas. Sometimes you will sit back and let your child work something out, rather than interfere. Even though you may be able to suggest a better method or improve your child's chances of success, you realise it is very important that she is allowed to try things out on her own and to learn from her own mistakes.

It is hard in an activity like this one to see precisely what is going to help the child and what will merely hinder her. It is not always possible to predict what will be the most effective way of helping her to work out her own solutions to a problem. We can plan activities in advance, and organise it so that children do specific tasks and have certain experiences. But at the end of the day, it is always more important to respond to a child's needs as they arise than it is to stick to a pre-decided plan.

Over 31
You enjoy doing things with your child and have a healthy respect for her ideas and opinions. You tend to listen first and then offer advice, which is a good way to encourage her to work out her own answers and solutions. You do need to be prepared to instruct her from time to time, and to share adult expertise on occasion. After all, it is not necessary for each generation to reinvent the wheel.

It is always very difficult to predict exactly which parts of any given task a child will find easy, and which parts she will struggle over. It is also hard to envisage which aspects of the whole activity will turn out to be relevant factors. For example, we might not have predicted that how many times the child is turned in a circle blindfolded would be relevant to how well she can remember objects on a tray. But for many children this turns out to be a major factor. It is the constant 'messiness' of any learning situation which makes it more important for a teacher to be able to *respond* effectively to a child's immediate needs, than to produce detailed advance plans.

POINTS TO REMEMBER

The National Curriculum outlines the subjects that children have to learn at each stage of their schooling. It does not tell teachers how they have to teach, but it does specify that they must produce a certain amount of written documentation as to both what they intend children to do, and how the children have got on.

It is open to question whether the emphasis which is laid on the advance planning and detailed reporting of teaching will, in fact, mean that actual teachers teach any better. At least one consideration has to be the fact that teaching is not the sort of job which can be broken down into a series of clearly defined stages or steps. Teaching seems to us to have more in common with parenting than it does with computer programming or building a house. Programming and house building are human activities requiring intelligence, care and, yes, even sensitivity, but they are not activities which require that houses or computers have to come to develop rights, duties, responsibilities and obligations.

CHAPTER FOUR

Testing and assessment

One of the questions most frequently asked about the National Curriculum is whether or not the children are going to be tested, and if so, at what ages.

Many of us remember tests from our own childhood. We may have memories of hushed classrooms, a list of questions and the feeling of rising panic. Some of us have seen our own children taking tests or exams and have felt for them as they struggle to remember facts and produce answers.

WHY TEST?

Tests can serve several purposes. They can be a means of selecting groups of children for different types of schooling. So, with the old 11+, certain children (those who passed) were selected to go to grammar schools, while others went to secondary moderns. Tests can be used to help a teacher decide which group or set a child should be in, so that they are working with other children who are about the same 'level of ability'. Sometimes, tests can be used to diagnose learning difficulties or to help us decide on the best work to give a child next. But there are problems.

Over the last thirty years there has been an increasing body of research giving evidence of the difficulties involved in any sort of testing. Suppose we test a group of thirty children. We find that ten are clever, ten are not so clever and ten seem to be pretty stupid. We put them into three groups and teach them accordingly. At the end of their schooling we have a look to see how they have done. We find that most of those who got to university or college came from the top set, that those in the bottom set got very few qualifications and tended to drop out of education early, and so on. Either the original test was accurate to the point of supernatural prophecy (if any test was *that* good there would be no need for professional testers), or the use of such tests was actually bringing with it its own problems.

The problem here is obvious. It is impossible to say that the difference in the children's educational success was due to the difference in intelligence. It could be due to the fact that the top set of children were told they were bright, expected to do well, made to feel confident, and perhaps, as the top set, had the more academically motivated teachers. By contrast, those who failed the test were told they were stupid, expected to do badly, not given hard or stimulating work, and were probably bored since nothing was expected of them.

Suppose the original group of children had been divided into three groups by a means other than a test, e.g. by their height or eye colour. Do you think the same thing would have happened? Those children, say the brown eyed ones, who were chosen as the 'bright' set, would have continued to do well. Whilst those children who were relegated to the bottom set, say the blue-eyed, would have started to fail. There is some evidence to suggest that this is what can happen.

So, tests can be self-fulfilling prophecies. If we tell children, or indicate to them, that we think they are bright and capable, that we expect them to do well, then the chances are that they will fulfill our expectations and shine. But if we tell children they are stupid, if we lower our expectations as to what they can do, they will lose confidence and start to fail.

WHAT IS A 'NORMAL' OR 'AVERAGE' CHILD LIKE?

We know, as parents, how difficult it is to say what is 'normal' development for a child. Some children cut their first tooth at three months and some at nearly one year. Both of these are 'normal'. In our house, Annie didn't take her first step until she was twenty months, while Fred was walking at ten months. Wilf, aged four and Matthew, aged two, are almost identically proficient on the climbing frame. Wilf is cautious and Matthew is foolhardy, but the development of both is well within the bounds of what we can normally expect.

Children develop at different rates and in different directions. As we commented in the previous chapter, they tend to grow in 'spurts' and this applies as much to what they learn and can do, as it does to their physical development. Just after Harry was brought a new pair of jeans, he grew two whole centimetres in one month. Similarly a child who expresses no interest in reading one day, and appears to have difficulty in recognising the word 'the', can be reading *Batman – The Movie* like a teenager the next week!

Trying to test children and then make

comparisons between them can be a nightmare when you take these factors into account. A child who can't do something one day, will appear to be a master of the skill the very next day. Even worse, a child who gets ten out of ten on a test can demonstrate a complete lack of understanding of the topic being tested in another situation ten minutes later. Frankly, we have never seen an 'average' child. If you ever find one then do him a favour by telling him that he could make a fortune in a career with the test designers.

It is difficult if not impossible to measure or test a child's ability or intelligence. We can invent tests or dream up testing situations, but these always tell us more about what we believe intelligence to be than they do about the child being tested. We cannot drill a hole into a child's head, take a torch and look to see if they really understand sentence structures, or how numbers work. We are not able to predict with any degree of accuracy just what any human being is capable of. Any parent can relate many stories of children who have surprised everyone, proving those who said they were stupid or unintelligent completely wrong. It is well known that Einstein demonstrated some brilliance in what he had to say in the theory of relativity. It is not so well known that his teacher thought him not particularly bright and that he got a poor degree from university.

WHAT WE CAN TEST

All that anyone – teacher, psychologist or parent – can do at the end of the day, is to look carefully at what a child can actually do. This may enable us to make judgements about what we *believe* a child can understand, but it still means that we have to watch what they actually *do*.

Basing our tests on what a child actually does in a given situation means basing them on some standard skill. Somewhere along the line someone has chosen some performance by a child as standard. Somewhere along the line the rest of us have given assent that some skill or performance will be an agreed criterion against which to compare other children's performances. Some years ago, in parts of British West Africa, a child would not be deemed ready for education until he could reach over his head with his right hand and touch his left shoulder. This was a quick base-line method for deciding whether or not a child was ready for school.

National Assessment is based on this very simple notion. We are not attempting to measure how much a child understands, or how clever she is, we are testing what she can actually *do*. National assessment is said, therefore, to concentrate upon 'performance'. This means that the 'tests' will look at what the children are doing, and then we will decide what level they have reached on the basis of which skills we see them using. For example, if a child is seen to be counting up to ten in order to thread some beads onto a string, we will know that she is at Level 1 in maths Attainment Target 2: 'Count . . . numbers up to 10'.

This means that the tests which are prescribed by the National Curriculum are not likely to look at all like the tests which most of us knew and loved in our own education. The tests will take days, maybe even weeks. They are supposed to take into account the children's ordinary classwork. They will involve the children in using a variety of skills: speaking, listening, explaining things to others, counting, measuring, investigating, predicting, estimating . . . to name but a few. Many of these skills will be practical and will need to be demonstrated through practical tasks. The entire collection of all the activities which go to make up this form of test will be called 'Standard Assessment Tasks' or SATs for short. These SATs will be administered to every child in the country at the key reporting ages of seven, eleven, fourteen and, eventually, sixteen.

CONTINUOUS ASSESSMENT

Teachers will be continually watching how children perform and recording their progress. They will be keeping a check as to which skills each child has acquired and which skills each child is having difficulty with. These records will be used to decide what level each child has reached in each subject. The final 'result' which we are given will have been obtained by looking at the evidence from not only the standard tests which every child does, but also at the teacher's own records.

FORMATIVE ASSESSMENT

The tests are different in another way from the old 11+ and similar tests used in the past. They are geared to help us to see where a child's weaknesses and strengths are, so that we can plan her future work efficiently. If we see that Raya has not yet acquired a particular skill, e.g. counting, we can take steps to help her to learn how to do this. This sort of testing, where we are looking to see what a child can and can't do in order to teach more effectively, is called 'formative assessment'.

SUMMATIVE ASSESSMENT

At regular intervals tests will also be used to provide a summary of what a child can and can't do. Teachers, and parents, will then be able to compare the levels which each child has reached in each part of each subject with the Levels they are expected to reach. Thus, seven-year-olds are expected to be at Level 2, eleven-year-olds are expected to be at Level 4. The summary will be reported to parents at the key reporting ages of seven, eleven, fourteen and sixteen.

WHAT PARENTS SHOULD AND SHOULDN'T DO

Because of the nature of these 'tests', it would be ridiculous to attempt to coach children so that they will 'pass'. Firstly, there is no question of 'failing', since the tests are really tasks designed to find out which Level the child has reached. Secondly, many of the tasks and activities included in the SATs will not be the sort of things which you can 'teach' children to do. They will not be paper and pencil excercises or the reproduction of memorised facts. So 'coaching' of the old-fashioned sort is unlikely to be very effective.

Remember that parents know much more about their children than the teachers. We have a good sense of what our children can do, and also of how they are getting on. It will pay to take a long-term view of all this continuous and standard assessment. If a child is not performing very well in a particular area at a given time, he may be developing in other areas or just due for a learning 'spurt'. What seems a big deal at the time, may prove to be a temporary hiccup in the long run.

Above all, it will be very sad for all our children's education if we take all this testing too seriously. Trying to say what a child can do, how much they know, still less what they are capable of, is all a bit of a mug's game really. It does not do to pretend that there is a sort of scientific truth about these assessments when they are at best human judgements. If we take it all too seriously we will be in danger of forgetting what the important things are – that children do grow and learn at different rates, that one human being can never finally predict what another human being can do or is capable of doing. Our best aim is to make useful, intelligent guesses.

Finally, national assessment can provide only 'base-lines' for deciding how well children are doing. In the educational career of any child, tests are always 'rules of thumb'.

ACTIVITY

You will need a pack of playing cards, and a pencil and paper.

While you and your child are sharing this activity, try to observe what your child does very closely. Notice what she can do and what she can't do; which skills she has and which skill she has trouble with. Although you should not apply any pressure, try to treat the activity as a sort of test!

Easy version

Draw a large triangle. Remove the kings, queens and jacks from the pack. Next, put aside all the aces, all the twos, all the threes, and one of the fours. Ask your child to put one of these cards in each corner of the triangle. Now ask her to choose a card from the remainder of the pack and put it in the middle. This card must have the same number of dots on it as the three cards on each corner of the triangle added together.

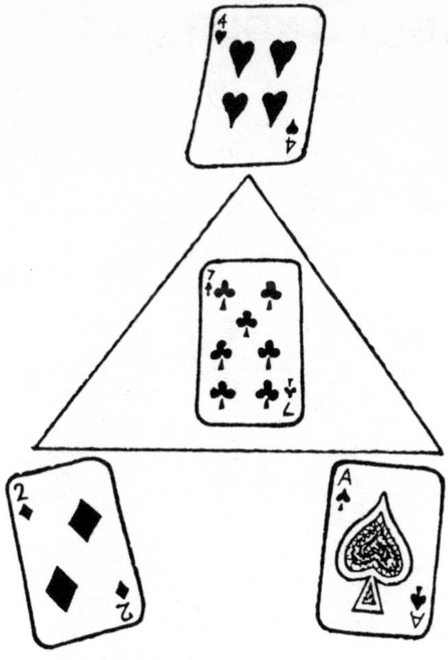

Let her have several goes at this. Can she do the same thing by throwing a dice three times and writing those numbers by the corners of the triangle?

Hard version

Draw a square. Ask your child to choose four numbers, one to be written on each corner. Keep the numbers low, depending upon the age of your child. Now ask her to add up the four numbers on each corner and write the correct answer in the middle of the square.

To make this even harder:

- try using large numbers;
- use a pentagon shape (five sides);
- start with the number in the middle and work out what numbers you could put around the edge.

QUIZ

1 Which parts of the activity did you pay most attention to?

(a) The counting or adding up.

(b) The choosing of the cards or numbers to go at the corners.

(c) Your child's talk.

(d) The choosing of the card or number to go in the middle.

2 Which parts of the activity did you offer most help with?

(a) The counting, number recognition or adding up.

(b) The choosing of the cards or numbers around the edge.

(c) The organisation of the whole activity.

(d) The choosing of the card or number to go in the middle.

3 What did your child enjoy most about this task?

(a) Talking to you.

(b) Counting or adding up.

(c) Playing with the cards.

(d) Looking at the shapes.

4 Which part did you think was the hardest?

(a) The counting or adding up.

(b) The choosing of the cards or numbers to go at the corners.

(c) The final selection of the middle number.

(d) Being organised by your child.

5 Which part of the task did you feel was most helpful to your child's learning?

(a) The mathematical parts.

(b) The talking and discussing parts.

(c) Having to make choices and sticking to them.

(d) Having to concentrate.

6 If you were to do this activity again with the same child, which of the following would you do?

(a) Make the numbers harder or the shape more complicated.

(b) Leave out any 'props' like cards.

(c) Let your child do it more on her own.

(d) None of the above, you felt it was a total waste of time.

7 If you had to give your child a mark out of ten for how she achieved on this task, how would you mark her?

(a) Give her nine out of ten on the basis that she tried hard and did as well as she could.

(b) Give her a mark based on how well you felt she counted, added, or knew her numbers.

(c) Give her a low mark on the basis that there are much harder versions of this task which she can't yet do.

(d) Impossible to mark her on a task like this.

SCORING YOUR QUIZ

	(a)	*(b)*	*(c)*	*(d)*
1	0	4	6	2
2	2	3	5	4
3	6	1	4	3
4	3	5	2	7
5	1	8	3	5
6	1	2	4	0
7	4	0	1	3

Under 15

When you were doing this activity with your child, you seemed to be looking out for certain things. You appeared to be fairly sure about the 'mathematical' skills that were required – counting, adding, recognising numbers, and so on. However, you were less convinced of the usefulness or importance of other sorts of skill – the negotiating as to who did what, the speaking and listening skills involved in the discussion and so on.

It is easy for adults, who have already acquired all these skills, to see them as separate rather than as very much connected. It may well be the case that a child's ability to talk things through is one of the factors which enabled her to count so efficiently. In another circumstance she may not have demonstrated her ability to do this at all. In a different situation, the way a child approaches a problem, the methods she uses, the procedures she tries and so on, will all be different. This does not matter at all in everday life. Children deal with problems as they arise and in the situation in which they find themselves. But it does matter when you are trying to test a child, because the circumstances set up by the task may well dictate whether or not the child can do the activity and can therefore be said to have acquired this or that skill.

16–29
You watched your child very attentively as she did this task. It seems that you were not too inclined to 'take over' or boss her around as she got on with it. This is all very helpful in encouraging children's learning and developing their own confidence.

You could see how your child needed to talk about what she did, and how important it was (and is) that she was comfortable in that learning situation. However, you were not so convincing that these factors played any part in whether your child could actually perform the mathematical procedures involved. Did the fact that your child talked all the way through the activity mean that she could count, when in another situation she might not have been able to do so? The research evidence is that this is indeed the case. Aspects of the situation and of the activity itself, which we have traditionally regarded as irrelevant to how children perform and to how well they can do particular sums, turn out to be anything but irrelevant. They turn out to be a part of the actual task itself.

Over 30
You and your child probably did a lot of talking to decide how this task should be organised and carried out. When you were watching your child you became aware just how important the role of talking and listening, organising the activity and laying down the 'rules' about how it should be carried out, were. At some level in yourself, you seem to realise instinctively that the 'mathematical' part of the activity – the counting, the number recognition, the adding up, and so on – cannot be separated from the rest of the task and the whole situation of which the child is a part. Factors which we might at one time have believed to be irrelevant to the 'test' or assessment, turn up and prove to be extremely relevant and, in some cases, are the deciding factors as to whether a child 'passes' or 'fails'.

This does not matter at all in everyday life. Children deal with problems as they arise and in the situation in which they find themselves. But it does matter when you are trying to test a child, because the circumstances set up by the task may well dictate whether or not the child can do the activity and therefore can be said to have acquired this or that skill.

POINTS TO REMEMBER

We now have a National Curriculum in England and Wales, and an important part of this is the fact that all children will be continuously assessed. This means that their progress will be recorded on the ten Levels of Attainment by the teacher. At intervals, parents will be given a summary of which Levels their children have reached in each area of each subject.

The four reporting ages at which the children's results will be made public are seven, eleven, fourteen and sixteen. The results produced will be based upon how the children do on the Standard Assessment Tasks (SATs), and also according to the teacher's own continuous records.

Testing children can be both difficult and can cause problems for later on. Therefore, the SATs do not look much like traditional tests. They are a series of tasks, many practical and involving talk, which the children do as a part of their normal classwork. The children should not realise that they are being tested.

It is very important that we do not allow the letter of the law to make us run away without our common sense. No test can be much good. At best, it can only give us a temporary indication of how a child is doing and what Level she has reached. It cannot give us any information as to what the child is capable of, how much she will learn in the next year, or of her intelligence. We must not take the assessment too seriously, and let it dictate what we expect of our children.

CHAPTER FIVE

What is maths?

At first sight this question seems stupid. We all remember being taught maths at school. If you stop an adult in the street, they will be able to give you a perfectly sensible answer to the question: 'Maths is about arithmetic, sums, tables, and so on.' Most people have memories of addition, subtraction, multiplication and division. Some can recall doing geometry or algebra. However differently we define maths, many of us would agree about what we thought of it at school: boring, hard, irrelevant, useless, even impossible! Exciting, creative, fun to do . . . were words more commonly applied to subjects like English or art. The proof of the pudding is in the eating, the result has been that few people continued their study of maths. Many of us dropped the subject as soon as they could – or even sooner! This goes for boys, and even more for girls.

MATHS IN HIDING

Although we may have given up the formal study of maths at school, it can be argued that we all went right on doing maths at home and at work. Sometimes we need to use a piece of 'school maths', such as when we are figuring out just how much money we are going to need to save each week in order to pay for Christmas. But more often the maths that we do as part of everyday life simply goes unrecognised. It is 'hidden' maths and we don't approach it in anything like the same way as school maths.

We may be having to organise a complicated day: 'I have to collect the baby from playgroup, then I must get to the supermarket . . . I've got to pick up the children from school, and there's the tea to cook . . . ' and I've got to pick up the prescription from the chemist . . . ' The way we solve such 'problems' may not feel much like the maths we did at school, but it does involve what are traditionally regarded as 'mathematical skills' – adding and subtracting times, estimating, calculating distances and speeds, and so on.

There has been some research done in America which followed women shoppers around the supermarket and looked at the ways in which they worked out the necessary sums. It was found that they often used their own 'unofficial' methods for working things out, rather than the methods taught in school.

NEW MATHS

Sometimes we don't recognise the 'hidden' maths. Indeed, when we were at school, it would not even have been thought of as 'proper' maths. Many of us will not have been taught the same things that our children are now learning in maths. For example, we were not taught to estimate either measurements or quantities at school. 'Guessing' simply was not a part of our mathematical experience. Indeed, one of us has abiding memories of a large and apparently fierce teacher shouting, 'Don't guess, child! Use your brain!' at a bewildered six-year-old.

Nowadays, the teacher will see estimation as an important skill. The National Curriculum explicitly requires that children are taught to estimate accurately and confidently. We encourage them to guess how long a particular rod is, or how tall that cupboard is. We ask them to estimate the answer of a sum or calculation *before* they actually work it out. This means that children have to think about what the right sort of answer is going to look like before they start the calculation, and it stops them making silly mistakes and then not realising they have made them. If Fred is asked to multiply 34×23, he may put a figure in the wrong column and get a ridiculous answer. But if he has been asked to estimate the answer first, he may be more inclined to realise that something is wrong.

APPLIED MATHS

Sometimes teachers speak of children having to 'apply' the mathematics they learn in school to 'real life' situations. Of course, children learn a lot of maths outside the school as well as inside it. Every time a mother tells her child that she has five minutes to get ready for bed before *EastEnders*, she is helping her child to develop an idea of what five minutes feels like.

It seems clear to us that children, and adults, need to use mathematical skills in many different situations. The ways in which they approach problems will depend upon the situation, as will the type of methods and strategies they use. Thus, to find out 'how many?', a child may count in one situation, they may estimate in another, and they may ask someone else in a third.

MATHS IN SCHOOL

When teaching maths in school, teachers have to be aware of the following:

- Children do better and are more inclined to learn if they are interested and confident. A bored or frightened child rarely makes a good learner, and one of the teacher's main tasks is to keep the children inspired and stimulated. If a child is motivated, it is astonishing what they are capable of learning at a very young age. Harry, in our house, spent hours and hours pouring over probability tables because they were a necessary part of his favourite role-playing game. Matthew, aged eighteen months can insert a video-tape into the machine and press the correct buttons to turn it on, in order to watch *The Snowman*!
- Once children leave the comparatively strange and sheltered environment of the classroom, the maths that they will require to enable them to function with efficiency and confidence will not come out of exercise books. Most work, and home, situations require that you think on your feet, calculate mentally, and are able to estimate with accuracy. They do not require that you work in a maths book, draw a margin down the left-hand side, and complete a page of neat sums.
- The National Curriculum will require that children can do a number of things which were simply not required of us when we were at school. Children will be asked to handle data, to develop a good sense of spatial awareness, to think investigatively and creatively about a mathematical problem, and so on. As teachers are planning their maths curriculum, they are bound to keep one eye on what the tests and tasks are going to ask children to do.

NOT JUST ONE WAY OF DOING THINGS

There has been a real change in education over the last fifteen years or so in terms of how teachers perceive problems in maths. There is no longer deemed to be one correct way of doing any sum, or approaching a problem. For many of us, memories of maths at school included being taught the 'right' way to do something, and if you did it another way then you were either stupid or sinful, ignorant or wicked! Now, the teacher will encourage children to explore a number of ways of doing any type of sum or calculation. As long as children can explain how they did it and can also come up with the right answer, the teacher is not so concerned with checking to see that they did it the 'right' way.

This has had the effect of making it possible for parents to confess their own 'personal' ways of doing maths, their private methods for getting an answer. These methods used to be kept hidden because many people were secretly ashamed that they were not using the 'correct' method that they had been taught at school. These 'private' methods, developed in the situations in which people find themselves outside the classroom, are now regarded as just as important and as much a part of 'real maths' as any other procedure.

To encourage children to develop mathematical skills in as many different contexts as possible, most teachers are now teaching at least a part of the maths curriculum, laid down by law, through what are called 'cross-curricular' tasks. These are activities which include some maths, some science, perhaps some history and some English and so on . . . This has the advantage that the number of contexts in which the child meets maths, at least in the classroom, has greatly increased. It enables the teacher to deliver a 'broad and balanced' curriculum and to motivate the children by setting mathematical tasks in situations that make sense in different areas of the curriculum.

ACTIVITY

You will need: A number of small pieces of paper with numbers clearly written on them. Some pieces of Sellotape.

The numbers you use can be as large or as small as you think your child can recognise. With very small children you can use dots instead of numbers.

Ask your child to choose a number and, without showing you what it is, stick it on your back. You then have to guess what it is. You may only ask questions which can be answered yes or no, for example:

- Is it larger than 3?
- Does it have a straight line in it?
- Is it the same as 2 add 4?
- Is it the same as your age?
- Is it less than the number of people in our home?
- Is it the same as the number of legs on the cat?

and so on. . .

Count how many questions you have to ask before you guess the number. Then change over. You choose a number and stick it on your child's back, who then has to guess it. How many questions does she have to ask?

The idea is to be as creative and imaginative as you like about all the questions.

QUIZ

1 As your child was doing this activity, did she enjoy asking the questions and talking about numbers?

(a) Not at all.

(b) Quite a lot.

(c) A great deal.

(d) Only for a few minutes.

2 Do *you* enjoy 'playing' or working with numbers?

(a) Not at all.

(b) Quite a lot.

(c) A great deal.

(d) Only in private and if nothing hangs on it.

3 When you were at school, what was your attitude to maths?

(a) It was one of your favourite subjects.

(b) It was a subject you liked but you couldn't stand the teacher.

(c) It was a subject you hated even though you were quite good at it.

(d) It was a subject you were bad at and disliked.

4 Would you say that discussing things like the shape of the number '6', the fact that the bus to school is 'number 12', or the way that most forks have four prongs, help a child's understanding of number?

(a) Not at all.

(b) Maybe, but you're not sure how.

(c) Yes, everything to do with numbers is bound to help.

(d) Only if the child doesn't already recognise their numbers.

5 In this activity, which of the following did your child do?

(a) Always copied your questions.

(b) Sometimes copied you.

(c) Never once copied your questions.

(d) Tried to copy you but failed.

6 Do you and your child talk about numbers as you go about the business of living your daily lives?

(a) Never.

(b) Very occasionally.

(c) Often.

(d) You don't know, you can't remember.

7 How would you describe a mathematician?

(a) Absolutely brilliant.

(b) No more intelligent than anyone else, it's just another skill.

(c) A certain sort of person (head in the clouds, impractical, etc.).

(d) Male.

SCORING YOUR QUIZ

	(a)	*(b)*	*(c)*	*(d)*
1	0	4	8	2
2	0	4	6	2
3	6	5	3	1
4	1	4	6	2
5	2	5	3	1
6	0	1	5	2
7	1	5	3	0

Under 15

You probably have never much liked maths and particularly number work, which has left you cold. However, you regard maths as an important subject, and you intend to put as much pressure on your children and offer them as much help as you possibly can. You still have a rather limited view of what maths is – or should be – about, and you see number work as a much more confined subject than it is in schools today. You have to be careful that your own negative feelings about the subject do not communicate through to your child. There is quite a bit of evidence that the parents' attitudes to a particular subject, especially maths, can affect how the child gets on in that subject. This is particularly true of girls and maths. If mother has decided that she hated maths at school, and that she is still not at all confident about it, then it is likely that her daughter will feel the same. 'I've always hated maths . . . never been any good at it. Even now, I can't seem to add four and four and get eight!', is hardly the sort of statement which is going to encourage a child, who looks up to her parents, to see maths as anything but boring, difficult and useless.

16–27

You appear to see yourself as reasonably confident in mathematics. You don't seem to have had an especially bad time with the subject at school and the very word maths does not strike fear into your heart or remind you of days of boredom at school. You enjoy maths around the home, and although you do not believe in pressurising your child unduly, you do see a role for chatting about numbers and helping your child make sense of maths as well as of language.

It is important to remember that numbers are not isolated or separable things.

You have never met a '2' walking down the street and neither have we. But 2, like any other number, is present in a large number of situations. Each one of those situations is a little bit different, and the way we cope with or manipulate the 2 will be a bit different as well. We need to deal with numbers as they arise and no conversation about numbers, no matter how bizarre or trivial, is ever wasted.

Over 28
You are clearly a confident person as far as maths goes. Perhaps you have a special gift in this direction, or perhaps you use specifically mathematical skills as part of your job. However it comes about, you are happy dealing with numbers and your child feels similarly.

You can see that the more talking there is about numbers, the more a child has to come to make sense of numbers and how they work. We can never separate numbers from the situation in which they occur, and it is very helpful for a child's mathematical development if mathematical ideas and skills are discussed, argued over and negotiated at home. The home is where children feel most confident, and it is likely to be where they give their best performances. We need to deal with numbers as they arise and no conversation about numbers, no matter how bizarre or trivial, is ever wasted.

POINTS TO REMEMBER

Children and adults learn maths in all sorts of situations – not only in the classroom between the hours of 9.00 am and 3.30 pm. We develop all sorts of mathematical techniques to cope with each situation as it arises. In schools, teachers are increasingly giving children a choice of method rather than insisting that they all do sums the same way.

We are aware that it is hard to say precisely where maths stops and where other subjects begin. It is equally difficult to draw a dividing line between those questions children ask which are relevant to their mathematical development and those which are not. It is easier to regard all questions as helpful and all information as grist to the mill. Conversations about numbers or any other aspect of maths which the children are interested in can only be helpful. At the end of the day, in maths as in everything else, it is a case of assisting children as they struggle to make sense.

CHAPTER SIX

How can you help?

Parents are not primarily teachers; at least not in the strict sense of the word. Of course, a mother or father can teach their child; indeed some of the most important skills that children acquire are taught by their parents, for example, crossing the road, tying their shoelaces, feeding themselves . . . to name but three.

PARENTS AND PARENTS

Parents do not see their main task in parenting as teaching, nor in helping their children become more knowledgeable. Parents are many things for their children including nurse, nanny, minder, rule-maker, policeman, food-provider, counsellor, friend and so on. Being a 'teacher' is one among many jobs. Although you may, on occasion, actually 'teach' your child to do a particular thing, like doing up buttons or crossing the road, most of what a small child learns is not like this. We have already talked about how children learn to talk simply by being immersed in language from (and before) day one. Much of the learning which happens at home is of this kind.

Children 'pick things up'; they learn that particular ways of behaving are associated with events that might happen. The kettle being switched on means that Mum is about to make tea. At a certain time of the day, Annie turns off the television. For some it will mean that Dad has supper ready. Children realise that they too can cause things to happen by starting a train of events. Matthew will often run out into the hall and ring the bell we keep by the phone.

He knows that this will cause all the other children to poke their heads out of their bedrooms or to come running down the stairs in the expectation of a phone call or visitor for them.

Small children are learning all the time. However, it would *not* be true that someone is teaching them all the time. Most of the time the role of the parent, or anyone else around, is that they simply 'enable' the child to learn by caring for them in a situation where learning is bound to take place. Sometimes teachers or even parents will talk as if we have to somehow persuade children to learn. It would be very hard, perhaps impossible, to *prevent* children from learning. The question is not so much *whether* they will learn, but rather *what* they will learn. It always seems to be true that one of the teenagers only has to let slip a swear word for the baby immediately to acquire it!

Since most things that we learn are not 'taught' to us directly, it seems appropriate that most of us spend only a small amount of time, as parents, teaching or instructing our children. Children do not need their parents to turn into teachers. They already have them at school. This is why the idea of 'Be Your Child's Best Teacher' is not one which the authors of this book share. We feel that parents have their own role to play in education and it is different from that of the teacher.

What then, is the role of the parent in a child's education? And in particular, what can parents do to help? In our experience the vast majority of parents are anxious that their children should do well at school and will do what they can to assist. Teaching your child how to do sums at home may not always be the best way of encouraging her to progress in maths. It can bore or confuse her. Yet sometimes a child may need more individual attention than she seems to be getting at school. How do parents know when to interfere, and when to leave well alone? If things are not going well, what can they do?

HOW PARENTS CAN HELP

1 Maths around the home

As we made clear in the last chapter, children can be developing mathematical skills and using mathematical techniques as they go about their own business (or other peoples!). As parents, we can support them in their struggle to make sense of what they are trying to do, or to work something out.

rying to work out from the es what time her favourite ping to be on. She cannot d the way the times are written and she gets confused between some of the days of the week. We can be of real assistance here, not simply by telling her when the film is on, and thus taking away her ability to organise it for herself, but instead, we can follow her struggles as she tries to work it out, and lend a hand at certain crucial moments. Perhaps we can point out to her that the hour comes first when they write the times, so that 7.35 is seven o'clock and a bit more. Perhaps we can help with the days of the week. If our aid is confined to fitting in with Annie's own working, then she learns a great deal more than if we *take over* the whole thing.

There are also situations at home where parents make the most of what is going on, in terms of talking about the maths involved. By and large, children learn to count because their mothers and fathers count with them, going up the stairs, putting on their coats, and so on. They come to recognise numbers because we point them out, 'There's a number 5 bus!' or 'Granny lives at number 12.'

Children will ask questions, and by answering these we can often help them to make connections or to realise how they can work something out. When Fred was little, he used to read the numbers of the houses on our side of the street. After a while he realised that these numbers went up in twos. He was tripping over himself with excitement as he told us this new and interesting fact. We pointed out to him that those on the other side of the street did the same. Then he realised that the two sets of numbers were related!

2 Games

Most children love playing games and benefit from the attention. Indeed, both card games and board games help to develop strategic thinking and practise arithmetical skills. When children are playing games they have to get the sums right because winning or losing depends upon it! Also they will often do a number of sums without complaint because they do not notice that they are doing them in the course of the game. The fun of playing together and the difficulty of having to learn how to lose as well as how to win, are good for much more than just the child's mathematical development.

There are some ideas for ways to adapt traditional card games and how to play them, at the end of this chapter.

3 Linking with school

This book comes out of the experiences we have had running a large project, IMPACT, through which parents are involved in their children's learning of maths in school. Many hundreds of parents are regularly sharing maths activities at home with their children, and though this does not always make for a quiet or easy life, it does mean that there is a lot of conversation about maths.

Even more parents are regularly involved in reading with their children, and in commenting upon what and how their children read. The conversa-

tion which parents have with their child's teacher, about the reading, is often a great help in making sure that the right sort of assistance is given to the child.

Parents rightly complain that the trouble with these types of schemes is that they depend upon the school and the teachers taking the initiative. If the school does not have any such policy of linking with the home, then it is difficult, if not impossible, for parents to do anything about it. However, most schools are keen that parents should support children's learning at home. If parents enquire about reading with their children, no teacher will fail to offer suggestions of ways to link with the work done in school. Similarly, asking how parents can best support the maths that the children are doing in class will enable the teacher to explain the best ways to help.

4 Setting the scene

We have already talked about how most of the things that children learn are not 'taught' but rather 'picked up'. Children do not, unfortunately, do what we *say*; they do as we *do*! If we want our children to take an interest in reading, then we have to show them that we value books, that we enjoy reading ourselves, that it is something that we choose to do, and make time for. If children never see their parents reading, then they are very unlikely to see the point of doing it, other than to please the teacher. It will not be seen an activity which anyone would choose to do for its own sake.

We show children by our actions much more powerfully than by our words, what activities we really value and consider important, and which ones we have no time for. Children who see their parents study, perceive study as worthwhile, as something that occupies their parents and for which space and time are made. If the most important item in the house is the television, and parents are rarely if ever seen with their noses stuck in books, children will pick up the clear message being given.

ACTIVITY

You will need: A pack of cards, some dice, perhaps some dominoes.

These are some suggestions as to games which can be played with children. They are good fun and also good practice for some number skills.

Cards

Pelmonism

This is a good game which can be

adapted to suit any child from the age of four to ten. Basically, either the whole pack of cards or some selection from it is spread out *face down* on the floor. The players then take it in turns to flip over two cards. If they are a pair (i.e. the same number), the player takes them out and keeps them. If they are not a pair, they are turned back over and left in the same place. The game continues until all the cards are taken,

To make this game easier for younger children, use only the cards below 6. To make the game harder, use the number cards plus the queens and aces. Then, a pair is defined as any pair of cards which add up to make ten, e.g. 4 + 6, 3 + 7, 2 + 8 and so on. Queens count as 0, aces as 1.

Fish

This is another good adaptable game. It is played by three or more people. Each person is dealt four cards, the remaining cards being put in a pile face down. The aim is to collect pairs, and this is done by each player asking one of the other players if they have a particular card: 'Have you got a two, Fred?' If the player being asked does have the required card, he must hand it over. If he does not have it, then he says 'Fish!', and the person asking must take one card off the central pile. Every time a player gets a pair, he places it in front of himself on the table. If a player runs out of cards, he picks up three more from the pile. At the end of the game, the player with the most pairs, wins.

To make this game very easy, use only the cards below 6 and deal only three cards each. To make it harder, use the number cards as well as queens and aces as described in the previous game. Players then collect pairs of cards which add up to ten.

Dominoes

Domino track

Ask your child to lay the dominoes in a long track. Can she do this so that all the ends of the dominoes match?

For older children, they could be asked to make a track in which all the ends add up to 6.

This is harder than it looks, especially if they have to try to use all the dominoes.

Domino square

Can your child lay the dominoes in a square so that all the corners match?

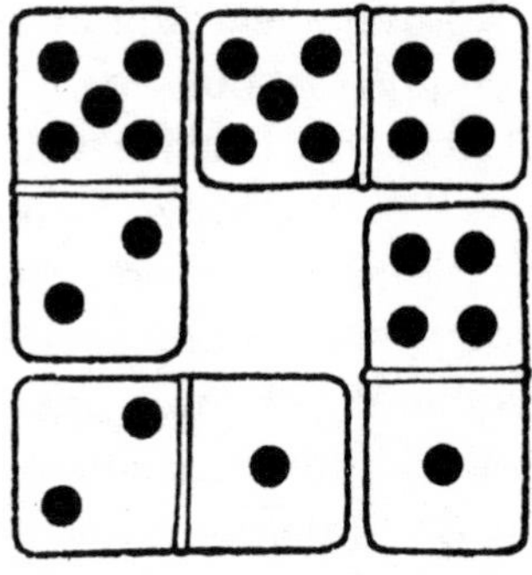

Can she make a square where the dominoes all add up to twenty?
What is the smallest number she can make a square add up to?

Dice

There are so many dice games and it is so easy to make up your own that it is impossible to choose even a representative selection.

Dicey races

Throw a dice a specified number of times, say three times. Add your scores. Let the other players have a go. Throw the dice again, three times. Continue to add on your score. At the end of five goes, the winner has the lowest score.

Variations on this idea include trying to get as close as possible to a given number, for example, twelve, but not going over. Therefore, you throw your three dice, and add the totals. If the answer is over twelve, you lose that turn's score; if it is under twelve, you add it on.

Or, invent some 'wild' numbers. For example, if you throw a six, you lose your score for that go. If you throw a two, your double your score for that go. If you throw ones, you lose your entire score and go back to zero . . . and so on!

Dice match-ups

Make games where you take it in turns to throw the dice, and you have to colour in that number of dots on a board. If you can't colour a space in, you have to take a counter. Keep playing until the first player has coloured all their spaces. The person with the most counters, wins.

To make this game harder, you can throw two dice and add the totals. You have to adapt your board. You can make it even harder by throwing two dice and finding the difference between the scores.

All of these games can be adapted. Children have great fun changing the rules and making up their own versions of games. This is very good for them, in that it means they have to think about the strategies involved. They also have to explain the rules of their new game in such a way so as to make sense to other people.

QUIZ

(Not to be embarked upon with an entirely straight face!)

1 How did you find this book?

(a) Informative.

(b) Lousy.

(c) About what you'd expect.

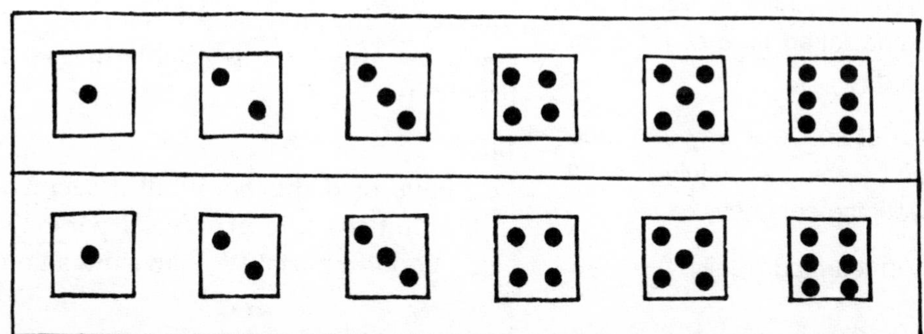

2 Which chapters did you like best?

(a) All of them.

(b) None of them.

(c) You can't remember, it was too long ago when you started reading the book.

3 How would you describe yourself?

(a) You're a good parent. You are quiet, patient, caring . . . in fact, nauseatingly perfect.

(b) You're a terrible parent. You are always shouting and you avoid your children – and other people's – whenever possible.

(c) You're not a parent at all. You're just nosey.

4 Which parts of the book did you enjoy the most?

(a) The quiz (extra marks for honesty).

(b) The activity (OK – parent of the year . . . !).

(c) The reading bit (liar or swot!).

5 How do you regard schools?

(a) Entirely necessary – how else will you keep the children out of the house and taken care of for eight hours a day?

(b) A waste of space – why can't the children be doing something useful like sweeping chimneys?

(c) Places of learning (really?!).

6 How have you found this quiz?

(a) Hilarious (swot!).

(b) Most unfunny (spoil-sport!).

(c) You don't know because you're not doing it (work it out!).

7 Would you read a sequel to this book?

(a) You must be joking.

(b) No.

(c) Only if written by someone else!

SCORING YOUR QUIZ

	(a)	*(b)*	*(c)*
1	8	1	3
2	6	0	2
3	3	1	6
4	7	3	1
5	6	3	0
6	8	1	110
7	0	0	0

Under 13
If you have read the book so far, you have either disagreed with large parts of it, or the things we have been saying have not yet sunk in! You can go back to the beginning and start again, *or* you could use the book as a table mat or a fire-lighter.

14–25
You have read this book but it seemed to be a bit like the proverbial parson's egg – good in parts! We said things you

could really agree with and get hold of, so to speak. But then, we would launch into something else you felt was much more worrying. At times the rug felt as if it was being pulled out from under your feet, and not very gently either! Don't give up. In twenty years you'll probably find the book is very useful with the grandchildren!

Over 26

OK, you've scored high again. You may be the clever-clogs who has read all the way through this book and has decoded exactly what we were getting at in each chapter, and fed us a diet of our own fodder in the quiz at the end of each chapter. This has guarenteed you high marks, but will it make you a better parent? Unless you are going for 'Parent of the year' award, you had better keep the book in a prominent place on the shelf for next year's revision!

Useful information

PACT — The London-based shared reading initiative.
Book: *Parent, Teacher, Child* by Alex Griffiths and Dorothy Hamilton. Methuen, 1984.
Book: *Learning at Home* by Alex Griffiths and Dorothy Hamilton. Methuen, 1987.

CAPER — *Children and Parents Enjoying Reading*
Book: CAPER: *Children and Parents Enjoying Reading* by Peter Branston and Michael Provis. Hodder and Stoughton, 1986.

Paired Reading — The Kirklees Paired Reading Project.
Book: *Peer Tutoring: A Handbook of Co-operative Learning* by Keith Topping. Croom Helm, 1988.

IMPACT — Maths with Parents And Children and Teachers.
Book: *Sharing Maths Cultures* by Ruth Merttens and Jeff Vass. Falmer Press, 1990.

HELPING YOUR CHILD AT HOME – SUGGESTED READING AND RESOURSES

The National Curriculum: A Survival Guide for Parents by Ruth Merttens and Jeff Vass. Octupus Books Ltd, 1989.

A Parent's Guide to Maths by Ruth Merttens. Octopus Books Ltd, 1987.

A Parent's Guide to Reading and Writing by Jane Salt. Octopus Children's Books, 1987.

Helping Your Child with Maths by Angela Walsh.

Activity Books in The Parent and Child Programme, by Ruth Merttens, Jane Salt and Louis Fidge. Octopus Children's Books, 1987–8.

BACKGROUND READING FOR THOSE INTERESTED IN PURSUING SOME OF THE IDEAS RAISED IN THIS BOOK

Bruner, J. (1983) *Child's Talk: Learning to Use Language* Oxford University Press.

Department of Education and Science (1967) *Children and their Primary Schools* (Plowden Report). HMSO.

Donaldson, M. (1978) *Children's Minds*. Fontana.

Hughes, M. (1986) *Children and Number*. Basil Blackwell.

Thomas, N. (1985) *Improving Primary Schools* (A Report of the Committee on Primary Education.) ILEA.

Tizard, B. and Hughes, M. (1984) *Young Children Learning*. Fontana.

Topping, K. and Wolfendale, S. (1985) *Parental Involvement in Children's Reading*. Croom Helm.

Wells, G. (1986) *The Meaning Makers: Children Learning Language and Using Language to Learn*. Hodder and Stoughton.

Wolfendale, S. (1983) *Parental Participation in Children's Development and Education*. Gordon and Breach Science Publishers.

Wood, D. (1988) *How Children Think and Learn*. Basil Blackwell.

Sewi…